Basil Hall Chamberlain

My Lord Bag-o'-Rice

Basil Hall Chamberlain

My Lord Bag-o'-Rice

ISBN/EAN: 9783744762892

Printed in Europe, USA, Canada, Australia, Japan

Cover: Foto ©Andreas Hilbeck / pixelio.de

More available books at **www.hansebooks.com**

MY LORD BAG-O'-RICE.

ONCE upon a time there was a brave warrior, called My Lord Bag-o'-Rice, who spent all his time in waging war against the King's enemies.

One day, when he had sallied forth to seek adventures, he came to an immensely long bridge, spanning a river just at the place where it flowed out of a fine lake. When he set foot on this bridge, he saw that a Serpent twenty feet long was lying there basking in the sun, in such a way that he could not cross the bridge without treading on it. Most men would have taken to their heels at so frightful a sight. But My Lord Bag-o'-Rice was not to be daunted. He simply walked right ahead,—squash, scrunch, over

the Serpent's body.

Instantly the Serpent turned into a tiny Dwarf, who, humbly bowing the knee, and knocking the planks of the bridge three times with his head in token of respect, said: "My Lord! you are a man, you are!

For many a weary day have I lain here, waiting for one who should avenge me on my enemy. But all who saw me were cowards, and ran away.

You will avenge

me, will you not? I live at the bottom of this lake, and my enemy is a Centipede who dwells at the top of yonder mountain. Come along with me, I beseech you. If you help me not, I am undone."

The Warrior was delighted at having found such an adventure as this. He willingly followed the Dwarf to his summer-house beneath the waters of the lake. It was all curiously built of coral and metal sprays in the shape of sea-weed and other water-plants, with fresh-water crabs as big as men, and water-monkeys, and newts, and tadpoles as servants and body-guards. When

they had rested awhile,
dinner was brought in
on trays shaped like
the leaves of water-
lilies. The dishes were
water-cress leaves,—not

real ones, but much more beautiful than real ones; for they were of water-green porcelain with a shimmer of gold; and the chopsticks were of beautiful petrified wood like black ivory. As for the wine in the cups, it *looked* like water; but, as it *tasted* all right, what did its looks signify?

Well, there they were, feasting and singing; and the Dwarf had just pledged the Warrior in a goblet of hot steaming wine, when thud! thud! thud! like the tramp of an army, the fearful monster of whom the Dwarf had spoken was heard approaching. It sounded as if a

continent were in motion; and on either side there seemed to be a row of a thousand men with lanterns. But the Warrior was able to make out, as the danger drew nearer, that all this fuss was made by a single creature, an enormous

Centipede over a mile long; and that
what had seemed like men with
lanterns on either side of it, were in
reality its own feet, of which it had
exactly one thousand

on each side of its
body, all of them glistening and
glinting with the sticky poison
that oozed out of every pore.
There was no time to be lost.
The Centipede was already half-way

down the mountain. So the Warrior snatched up his bow, a bow so big and heavy that it would have taken five ordinary men to pull it,—fitted an arrow into the bow-notch, and let fly.

He was not one ever to miss his aim. The arrow struck right

in the middle of the monster's forehead. But alas! it rebounded as if that forehead had been made of brass.

A second time did the Warrior take his bow and shoot. A second time did the arrow strike and rebound; and now the dreadful creature was down to the

water's edge, and would soon pollute the lake with its filthy poison. Said the Warrior to himself: "Nothing kills Centipedes so surely as human spittle." And with these words, he spat on to the tip of the only arrow that remained to him (for there had been but three in his quiver). This time again the arrow hit the Centipede right in the middle of its forehead. But instead of rebounding, it went right in and came out again at the back of the creature's head, so that the Centipede fell down dead, shaking the whole country-side like an earth-quake, and the poisonous light on its two thousand feet darkening to a dull glare like that of the twilight of a stormy day.

Then the Warrior found himself wafted back to his own castle; and round him stood a row of presents, on each of which were inscribed the words "From your grateful Dwarf." One of these presents was

a large bronze bell, which the
Warrior, who was a religious
man as well as a brave
one, hung up in the
temple that con-
tained the tombs
of his ancestors.

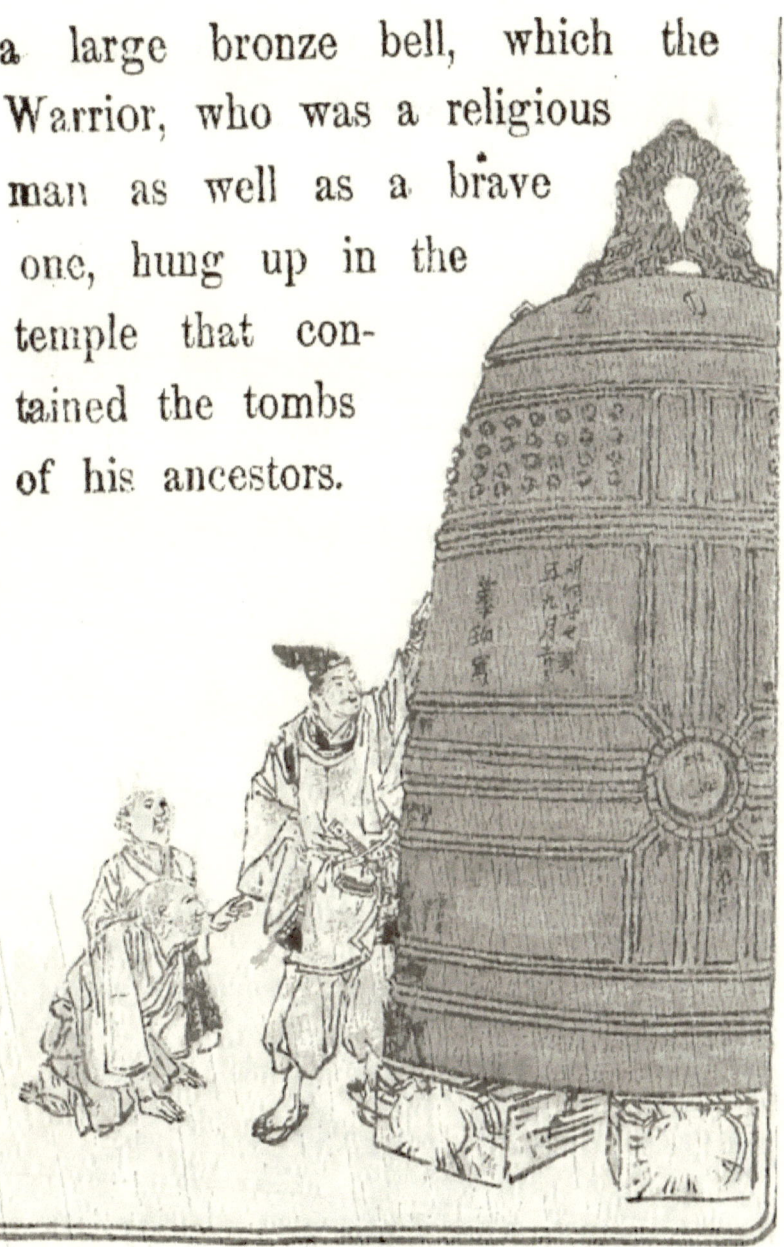

The second was a sword, which enabled him ever after to gain the victory over all his enemies. The third was a suit of armour

which no arrow could penetrate.

The fourth was a roll of silk, which never grew smaller, though he cut off large pieces from to time to make himself a new court dress.

The fifth was a bag of rice, which, though he took from it day after day for meals for himself. his family and his trusty retainers, never got exhausted as long as he lived.

And it was from this fifth and last present that he took his name and title of

"My Lord Bag-o'-Rice;"

for all the people thought that there was nothing stranger in the whole world than this wonderful bag, which made its owner such a rich and happy man.

Told in English for Children by B. H. Chamberlain.

明治二十二年九月廿八日版權免許

人

發兌書肆

長谷川武次郎

東京日本橋區通鹽町三番地

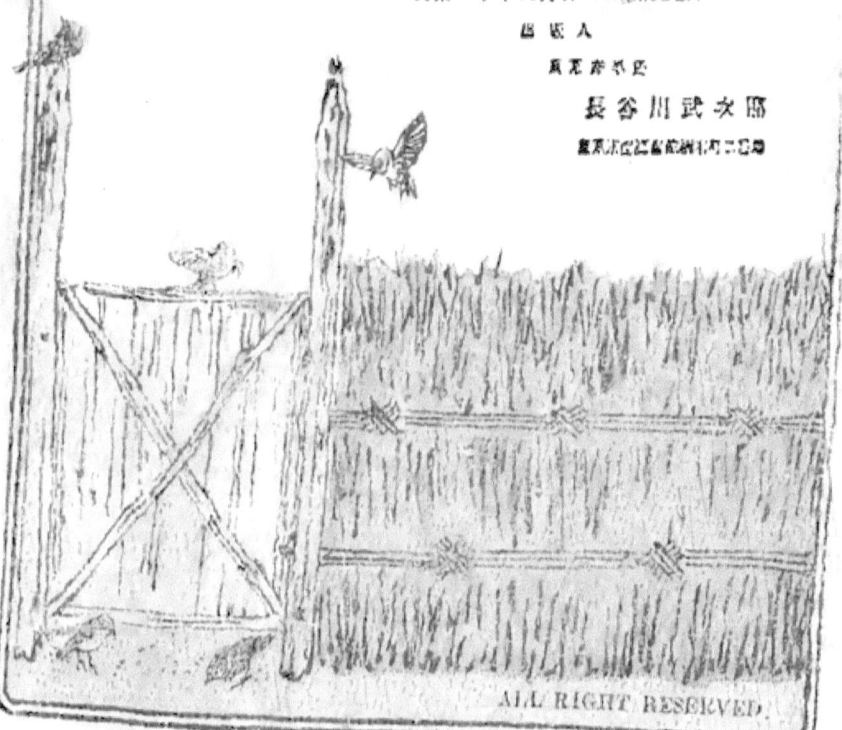

Printed by the Kobunsha in Tokyo, Japan.